Date: 7/2/21

J BIO OSAKA
Scarbrough, Mary Hertz,
Naomi Osaka /

NAOMI OSAKA

Women in Sports

MARY HERTZ SCARBROUGH

Rourke
Educational Media

A Division of
Carson Dellosa Education

Before Reading: *Building Background Knowledge and Vocabulary*

Building background knowledge can help children process new information and build upon what they already know. Before reading a book, it is important to tap into what children already know about the topic. This will help them develop their vocabulary and increase their reading comprehension.

Questions and Activities to Build Background Knowledge:

1. Look at the front cover of the book and read the title. What do you think this book will be about?

2. What do you already know about this topic?

3. Take a book walk and skim the pages. Look at the table of contents, photographs, captions, and bold words. Did these text features give you any information or predictions about what you will read in this book?

Vocabulary: *Vocabulary Is Key to Reading Comprehension*

Use the following directions to prompt a conversation about each word.

- Read the vocabulary words.
- What comes to mind when you see each word?
- What do you think each word means?

Vocabulary Words:
- descent
- diversity
- introvert
- serve
- sets
- sponsors

During Reading: *Reading for Meaning and Understanding*

To achieve deep comprehension of a book, children are encouraged to use close reading strategies. During reading, it is important to have children stop and make connections. These connections result in deeper analysis and understanding of a book.

 Close Reading a Text

During reading, have children stop and talk about the following:

- Any confusing parts
- Any unknown words
- Text to text, text to self, text to world connections
- The main idea in each chapter or heading

Encourage children to use context clues to determine the meaning of any unknown words. These strategies will help children learn to analyze the text more thoroughly as they read.

When you are finished reading this book, turn to the next-to-last page for **After Reading Questions** and an **Activity**.

TABLE OF CONTENTS

A WOMAN OF THREE COUNTRIES

Naomi Osaka was born in 1997 in Japan, her mom's home country. When she was a toddler, her father saw tennis legends Venus and Serena Williams on television. He thought Naomi and her older sister, Mari, could do that. Naomi was regularly hitting tennis balls by age three.

Sisterly Competition

Naomi says she was motivated by the challenge to beat her sister, not by the game itself. Every day she said to her sister, "I'm going to beat you tomorrow," she told a reporter in 2018. It took her 12 years to do it.

Naomi's dad is Haitian. Her mom is Japanese. The family moved from Japan to the state of New York when Naomi was three. They lived with her grandparents until 2006. Then, the family moved to Florida.

Naomi is of Japanese and Haitian **descent**, but she was also raised in the United States. She says she identifies with all three countries.

descent (di-SENT): the origin, background, or nationality of someone's family

AN UPCOMING ACE

When Naomi started playing tennis professionally in 2013, she had to decide which country she would represent.

Her parents felt Japan was more focused on Naomi. They wanted her to have lots of opportunities for growth and **sponsors**. Even though Naomi represents Japan, she still lives and trains in the U.S.

sponsors (SPAHN-surs): people or organizations that support an event, activity, or person, usually with money

The Women's Tennis Association (WTA) ranked Naomi 430th in the world at the end of 2013. A year later, she was still ranked in the 400s when she defeated Samantha Stosur, winner of the 2011 U.S. Open. It was Naomi's third WTA tournament. Samantha was ranked 19th in the world at the time.

Naomi's hard work began to pay off in 2016. That year, she played in three Grand Slam tournaments. In September, she made it to her first WTA final. She was ranked 40th in the world at the end of 2016. The WTA named her Newcomer of the Year.

The Grand Slam Tournaments

The Grand Slam is a series of famous and well-respected tennis tournaments. The four tournaments are the Australian Open, the French Open, Wimbledon (in England), and the U.S. Open.

Naomi is 5 feet 11 inches (180 centimeters) tall and right-handed. Her **serve** is one of the fastest in women's tennis. It's been measured at over 125 miles (201 kilometers) per hour. Such a fast serve can result in an ace. An ace is a serve that the other player doesn't hit back; it counts as a point.

serve (surv): to begin play in tennis by hitting the ball over the net

Naomi won her first professional title in March of 2018 at a major tournament in California. Later that month in Miami, Florida, she faced Serena Williams, her childhood idol and one of the best players to ever step on a tennis court.

Naomi won two **sets** against Serena, securing a win and moving forward. However, she later lost a match in the same tournament.

sets (sets): groups of games in a tennis match

Learn the Lingo: Game, Set, Match

In women's tennis, the player who wins the best of three sets wins the match. To win a set, a player must win at least six games. The game points are called love, 15, 30, and 40.

When she was in the third grade, Naomi wrote a report about Serena Williams, shown above.

In September of 2018, Naomi would play Serena again. This time, they were in the U.S. Open final.

The match was filled with ups and downs. Serena and the referee argued, and she was given several penalties. Naomi won, taking home her first Grand Slam title at age 20. She says the victory was "bittersweet."

Biggest Supporters

Serena shared a message that Naomi had sent after the match: "People can misunderstand anger for strength because they can't differentiate between the two. No one has stood up for themselves the way you have, and you need to continue trailblazing."

While the match against her idol did not go as planned, winning the 2018 U.S. Open made Naomi Japan's first Grand Slam champion. She's likely the first Grand Slam champion of Haitian descent as well.

In early 2019, Naomi was ranked the number one women's player in the world.

Represent!

Reporters often ask Naomi about her Japanese background. They sometimes forget about her Haitian connection. She always stresses its importance. She says, "I just feel like me."

In January 2019, Naomi won her second Grand Slam title at the Australian Open. Once again, the final was intense.

Naomi lost at the 2019 U.S. Open. But, she made headlines for her kindness to opponent Coco Gauff. The 15-year-old player described Naomi as a true athlete—an enemy on the court and a best friend off of it.

Coco defeated Naomi at the Australian Open in January 2020.

OFF THE COURT

Though she is a Japanese citizen, Naomi understands Japanese better than she speaks it. She often listens to reporters' questions in Japanese and replies in English. Naomi describes herself as an **introvert** and says her shyness and perfectionism sometimes make her nervous about speaking Japanese in public.

introvert (IN-truh-vurt): a shy person who does not share thoughts or feelings easily

Gotta Catch 'Em All!

News reports often mention Naomi's quirky sense of humor. She once explained that her goal is, "To be the very best. Like no one ever was." Then, she had to explain that she was just quoting the Pokémon theme song!

As the first Asian tennis player to reach number one in the world, Naomi has become popular in Japan. Her fame has highlighted some issues with **diversity** in Japan. An advertisement from one of her sponsors showed her with clearly lighter skin than her natural skin tone. They had to remove it.

Naomi has since asked her sponsors to get permission from her about the way they use her image.

diversity (di-VUR-si-tee): the inclusion of people who are different from each other

Naomi believes that being a role model is a "huge responsibility" and that inspiring young girls who want to play tennis is "one of the best things that I could possibly do in life."

Naomi plans to represent Japan in the Olympic Games. Fans from all over the world will be cheering for her.

A subway station in Tokyo, Japan, features Naomi's image.

Memory Game

at the pictures. What do you remember

ng on the pages where each image appe

Index

Text-Dependent Questions

1. Did your understanding of what it takes to be one of the greatest athletes in the world change after reading this book? Explain.

2. What do you think makes Naomi successful and inspiring?

3. Which Grand Slam tournaments has Naomi won?

4. How do you think Naomi has been influenced by her Haitian, American, and Japanese connections?

5. Naomi's idol is Serena Williams. Who is someone that you admire and want to be like?

Activity

Naomi had to make the difficult choice of which country to represent in international competitions. If you were in her situation, what would help you decide? Would you want your parent, coach, or others to decide for you? Why or why not? Write your thoughts in a journal entry.

About the Author

Mary Hertz Scarbrough is enormously impressed with Naomi Osaka's dedication to and success in tennis. She also appreciates Naomi's quirky sense of humor and grace under pressure. She lives in South Dakota and chases her two rescue dogs, rather than tennis balls, when she's not writing.

www.rourkeeducationalmedia.com

Quote sources: Larmer, Brook, "Naomi Osaka's Breakthrough Game," the New York Times, August 23, 2018: https://www.nytimes.com/2018/08/23/magazine/naomi-osakas-breakthrough-game.html ; BBC Sport, "Naomi Osaka: US Open title 'not the happiest moment' after Serena Williams' outbursts," BBC, October 1, 2018: https://www.bbc.com/sport/tennis/45711180 ; Williams, Serena, "Serena Williams Poses Unretouched for Harper's BAZZAR," Harper's BAZZAR, July 9, 2019: https://www.harpersbazaar.com/culture/features/a28209579/serena-williams-us-open-2018-essay/ ; Gregory, Sean, "Tennis Star Naomi Osaka Doesn't Like Attention. She's About to Get a Ton of It," TIME Magazine, January 10, 2019: https://time.com/5498898/naomi-osaka/

PHOTO CREDITS: page 4-5: Shutterstock; page 6-7: Shutterstock; page 9: Shutterstock; page 11: Shutterstock; page 12-13: Shutterstock; page 14: Shutterstock; page 15: Shutterstock; page 17: Shutterstock; page 18-19: Shutterstock; page 20-21: Shutterstock; page 22-23: Shutterstock; page 24-25: Shutterstock; page 26-27: Shutterstock; page 28-29: Shutterstock

Edited by: Madison Capitano
Cover and interior design by: Rhea Magaro-Wallace

Library of Congress PCN Data

Naomi Osaka / Mary Hertz Scarbrough
(Women in Sports)
 ISBN 978-1-73163-828-1 (hard cover)
 ISBN 978-1-73163-905-9 (soft cover)
 ISBN 978-1-73163-982-0 (e-Book)
 ISBN 978-1-73164-059-8 (ePub)
Library of Congress Control Number: 2020930208

Rourke Educational Media
Printed in the United States of America
01-1942011937